In Our Neighborhood

Meet a Teacher!

by AnnMarie Anderson

Illustrations by Lisa Hunt

Children's Press®
An imprint of Scholastic Inc.

MSCHOLASTIC

Special thanks to our content consultants:

Christine Harris
Retired Elementary Teacher
   and Assistant Principal
Massapequa Public Schools, Massapequa, NY

Jackie Fego
Elementary Teacher
C.V. Starr Intermediate School
Brewster, NY

Library of Congress Cataloging-in-Publication Data
Names: Anderson, AnnMarie, author. | Hunt, Lisa, 1973– illustrator.
Title: Meet a teacher!/by AnnMarie Anderson; [illustrations by Lisa Hunt]
Other titles: Meet a teacher!
Description: New York: Children's Press, an imprint of Scholastic Inc., 2021. | Series: In our neighborhood |
   Includes index. | Audience: Ages 5–7. | Audience: Grades K–1. | Summary: "This book introduces readers
   to the role of teachers in our community"— Provided by publisher.
Identifiers: LCCN 2020033787 | ISBN 9780531136843 (library binding) | ISBN 9780531136904 (paperback)
Subjects: LCSH: Teachers—Juvenile literature. | Teaching—Juvenile literature.
Classification: LCC LB1775 .A4793 2021 | DDC 371.1—dc23
LC record available at https://lccn.loc.gov/2020033787

Produced by Spooky Cheetah Press
Prototype design by Maria Bergós/Book & Look
Page design by Kathleen Petelinsek/The Design Lab

Printed in North Mankato, MN, USA 113

1 2 3 4 5 6 7 8 9 10 R 30 29 28 27 26 25 24 23 22 21

Scholastic Inc., 557 Broadway, New York, NY 10012.

Photos ©: 7: Monkey Business Images/age fotostock; 9: Bob Daemmrich/Alamy
Images; 13: Digital Vision/Getty Images; 17: Monkey Business Images/Dreamstime;
19: Yellow Dog Productions/Getty Images; 20: Adam Hester/Getty Images;
23: Christian Science Monitor/Getty Images; 24 left: William Garcia/Alamy Images;
24 right: Jill Toyoshiba/Kansas City Star/Tribune News Service/Getty Images; 25 left:
David Grossman/Alamy Images; 25 right: SDI Productions/Getty Images; 31 bottom
left: Tatyana Abramovich/Dreamstime; 31 bottom right: Jamie Pham Photography/
Alamy Images.

All other photos © Shutterstock.

Table of Contents

Our Neighborhood. 4

Meet Mr. Garcia 6

Lunchtime! 16

A Fun Afternoon 20

▶ Ask a Teacher 28

▶ Mr. Garcia's Tips. 30

▶ A Teacher's Tools 31

▶ Index. 32

▶ About the Author 32

OUR NEIGHBORHOOD

Hi! I'm Emma. This is my best friend, Theo. Welcome to our neighborhood!

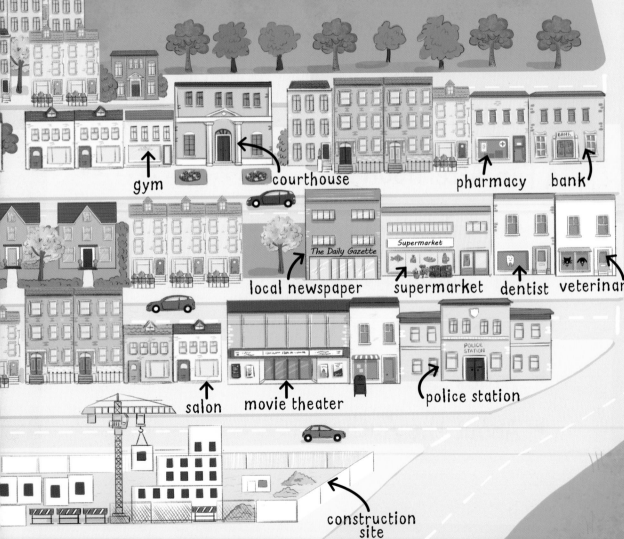

gym

courthouse

pharmacy

bank

local newspaper

The Daily Gazette

Supermarket

supermarket

dentist

veterinarian

salon

movie theater

POLICE STATION

police station

construction site

recycling center

fire station

hospital

restaurant

library

post office

café

school

Our school is right there. Today was a special day. I won a writing contest and was picked to be teacher for a day!

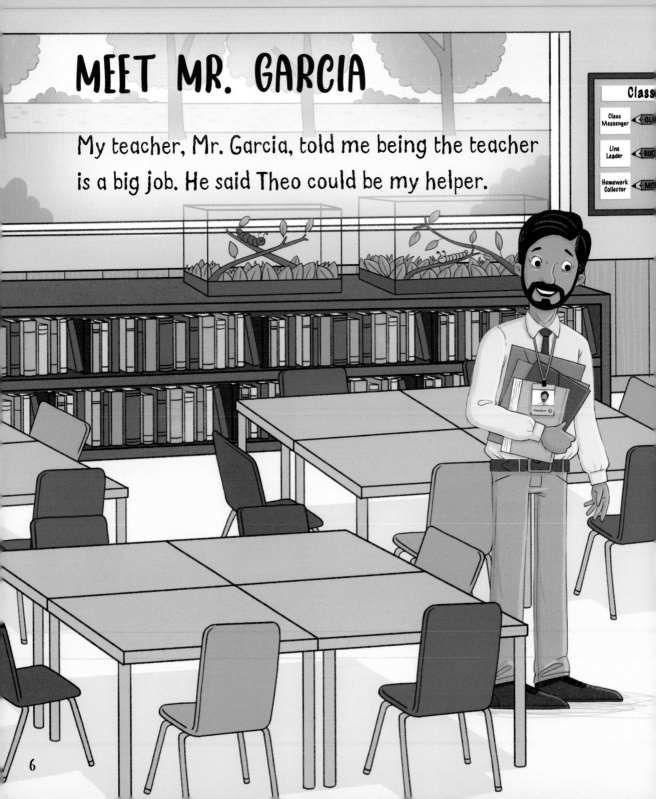

MEET MR. GARCIA

My teacher, Mr. Garcia, told me being the teacher is a big job. He said Theo could be my helper.

First we had our morning meeting. I took attendance.

Is Jackson here?

Good morning, Emma!

Some classrooms have a teacher's aide to help the teacher. In other classrooms there may be a student teacher. That is someone who is studying to be a teacher.

m Helpers

Class Messenger ← GUS

Pet Helper ← SABINE

Plant Helper ← JOSE

Everyone in our class has a job, like line leader or homework collector. After attendance, I assigned classroom helper jobs for the week.

Please bring this to the office.

Classroom Helpers

Class Messenger	← OLIVIA	Class Messenger	← GUS
Line Leader	← RODNEY	Pet Helper	← SABINE
Homework Collector	← MOLLY	Plant Helper	← JOSE

Then I asked the class messengers to take the notes from home to the main office.

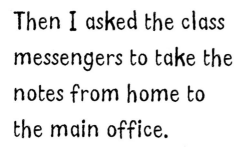

The school principal's office is usually near the main office. The principal is the school's leader. The principal's job is to support the teachers and the students.

We have four different "specials" classes each week. There is a different teacher for each one.

Art teachers show students how to express themselves creatively. They may use paint, clay, markers, paper, and other materials.

Physical education teachers show kids how to play various sports and games. They teach students to work as a team and stay healthy and fit.

Library media specialists are teachers and librarians. They help students find information in the library. They also teach technology and help kids pick a "just right" book.

Music teachers are teachers and musicians. They teach musical ideas like tempo, pitch, and rhythm.

Today our class had music.

While our classmates were at music, Theo and I went back to the classroom with Mr. Garcia for his prep period. During that time, he prepares lessons, calls students' caregivers, and grades homework.

We're going to make a bar graph in math today.

FALL LEAVES

NUMBER OF LEAVES

15

10

5

0

RED   ORANGE   YELLOW   BROWN

I love graphing!

Teachers meet with students' parents or caregivers once or twice each year. They talk about how the student is doing in class. Sometimes students join, too.

Mr. Garcia and Theo helped. We each led one group.

I loved that character, too!

Teachers review and grade their students' work. It is a teacher's job to make sure students understand what they have learned.

Room Helpers

Class Messenger → GUS

Pet Helper → SABINE

Plant Helper → JOSE

LUNCHTIME!

It was finally lunchtime! Theo and I led our class to the cafeteria. Mr. Garcia explained how he sometimes has lunch duty.

Mr. Garcia, can you please open my milk?

He makes sure everyone is following the cafeteria rules and helps any students who might need it.

Of course!

Teachers get a break from duties, too. That's usually when they eat lunch. Sometimes teachers use part of their time to meet with or help students.

After lunch, we went outside for recess. Mr. Garcia made sure everyone stayed safe on the field and playground. He said Theo and I could take a break. We went to play on the swings.

Teachers are also there to offer support. If a student feels sad or alone, a teacher can often help.

I can help with that!

I don't have anyone to play with.

A FUN AFTERNOON

When we got back to class, it was time for math. Mr. Garcia showed me how to use the interactive whiteboard to lead the lesson.

Many teachers use interactive whiteboards. The teacher and students interact with computer graphics on a touch screen.

I called Marlow up to the board. I asked her to show the number of orange leaves on the bar graph. She did a great job!

FALL LEAVES

How many orange leaves are there?

Four!

F LEAVES

15

10

0

RED   ORANGE   YELLOW

Then it was time for my favorite subject: science! We were studying the life cycle of butterflies. Theo and I called our classmates over to the tanks, one table at a time. Everyone checked their caterpillars. Then they returned to their desks to draw pictures showing how much the caterpillars had grown.

Mine should be ready to form a chrysalis soon!

Class

Class Messenger

Line Leader

Homework Collector

Teachers are always learning—just like students! They share ideas with other teachers. They attend conferences and take classes to learn how to be better teachers.

23

While the others were working, Theo and I had a chance to talk to Mr. Garcia. I told him I never realized how much teachers do! Theo asked what other jobs there are at a school. Mr. Garcia was happy to explain.

Crossing guards stop traffic. They help children get across the street safely on their way to and from school.

School nurses treat illnesses and injuries. They also help students stay healthy and ready to learn while at school.

Custodians keep the classrooms—and the rest of the school—clean.

Bus drivers get students to and from school safely each day. They also transport kids on field trips.

Wow. A lot of people work at our school!

At the end of the day, Mr. Garcia volunteered for bus duty so he could show us how that worked. We made sure everyone got on the right bus to go home. Theo and I helped Mr. Garcia check names off the list. Then it was finally time for us to go home.

"That was a lot of fun," I said. Theo agreed. We also agreed that being a teacher is hard work!

Ask a Teacher

Theo asked Mr. Garcia some questions at the end of the day.

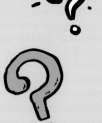

Why did you become a teacher?

I have always loved learning and loved children. I knew becoming a teacher would give me an opportunity to keep learning and to share that learning with my students.

How many years did you train to become a teacher?

I went to college for four years. Then after I became a teacher, I had to get a master's degree, which took another two years. Teachers must also continue to take teaching classes.

What is the hardest part of your job?

It's hard to find time in the day to fit in all the fun things I have planned.

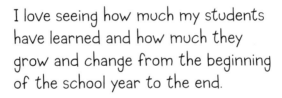

What is the best thing about being a teacher?

I love seeing how much my students have learned and how much they grow and change from the beginning of the school year to the end.

What advice would you give someone who wants to become a teacher?

A good teacher should make a connection with students and make them feel good about themselves and their schooling.

Mr. Garcia's Tips for a S.M.A.R.T. Classroom

Stay safe!

Make good choices and be thoughtful.

Arrive on time, prepared, and ready to learn.

Respect yourself, your classmates, your teacher, and your school.

Try your best!

A Teacher's Tools

Dry erase board: Teachers use these boards to post important information, such as homework assignments, sight word lists, and more.

Computer: Teachers can use this electronic machine to take attendance, create lesson plans, and email parents.

Math manipulatives: Teachers use these objects to teach math concepts like addition and subtraction.

Classroom library: Teachers share this collection of books with their students.

Index

bus drivers 25
bus duty 26
classroom helper
   jobs 8, 9
classroom
   library 31
computer 31
conferences 23
crossing guards 24
custodians 25
dry erase board 31
grading students'
   work 12, 15

homework 8, 12, 31
interactive
   whiteboard 20,
   21
language arts 14,
   15
lunchtime 16, 17
main office 9
math 12, 20, 21
math
   manipulatives 31
parent-teacher
   meetings 13

prep time 12
principal 9
recess 18, 19
school nurses 24
science 22, 23
specials 10, 11
student teacher 7
support 19
teacher 6, 7, 9, 10,
   11, 13, 15, 17, 19, 20,
   23, 24, 27, 28, 29,
   30, 31
teacher's aide 7

About the Author

AnnMarie Anderson has written numerous books for young readers—from easy readers to novels. She lives in Brooklyn, New York, with her husband and two sons. Her mom is a retired schoolteacher and assistant principal.